How to Write a Perfect Wedding Speech

The Ultimate Wedding Toast Guide

Madison Jeffrey

D1714587

Copyright

© 2012 by Madison Jeffrey

ISBN: 978-1-304-70593-8

Terms of Use

Any information provided in this book is through the author's interpretation. The author has done strenuous work to reassure the accuracy of this subject. If you wish you attempt any of the practices provided in this book, you are doing so with your own responsibility. The author will not be held accountable for any misinterpretations or misrepresentations of the information provided here.

All information provided is done so with every effort to represent the subject, but does not guarantee that your life will change. The author shall not be held liable for any direct or indirect damages that result from reading this book.

Contents

Introduction

Many people have problems about giving speech in public because they are not used to on the task. People fear to talk in front of many people because they are afraid that they would make mistakes and just make a fool of themselves. But we have the obligation to do it because it is expected from us. One example would be during a wedding ceremony.

Wedding ceremony is the time where every close relative of the groom and bride are expected to give their congratulatory speech. Some of them may do it willingly but others will be hesitant because they do not know how to make a speech that will enjoy by the people and welcomed by the bride and groom.

Creating a speech can be a hard task when you have never tried giving one. It can also be very difficult when you are not used to writing one. Fortunately, this guide is made to solve the problem. This will be your ultimate guide towards writing and giving speeches that will be remembered by everybody.

You will be learning about how you should write a speech, how to give them in front of many people and many more related things. The guide will also teach you how to relax and have confidence when you are in front with so many people giving the speech. You can also read some examples of speeches that you can use as an idea of making your own one. It will be yours to decide.

So, let your speech be an inspiration of the newlywed couple. Weddings are supposed to be enjoyed and celebrated for the two people in loved with each other and not being afraid and anxious towards giving the speech. This time, things like that won't happen in the future. You are given the privilege here in this guide to load yourself with techniques of how to give speeches in front of many people. So, start your way now!

When Does Wedding Speeches and Toasts Started?

Past traditions of wedding speeches and toasts were for the fathers of the bride and groom, also sometimes the groom. Brides were not given the chance to have their own thoughts about their wedding in front of many people. It was not really a part of the culture but it was just to meant like that.

The speeches made long ago differ from each other. In Egypt, the speeches were all about blessings and offerings to the gods of people for having the ceremony. In Europe, the fathers of both side talked about the great unions between both families. But for Ireland, England and Scotland mothers gave blessings and toasts during the wedding day.

There are other cultures that did not involve the bride and groom. Celebrations were still part of the wedding but the traditions were slowly changing. Some of the traditional people who must give speeches were taken away. In the past, maid of honor didn't deliver speech but as of today, it is now very common. The new traditions and cultures of wedding ceremonies now have greatly changed. Some may still be there but there are new added ones.

This guide is not about the wedding traditions. It will talk about wedding speeches to teach you and give some idea. Wedding speeches have changed for many years now. Modern wedding speeches have greatly evolved, adding some humors plus the wishes for the bride and groom.

But it's good to know a little history about wedding speeches and who were the people giving them long ago. If you are one of those people who are assigned to give speech on wedding day, here is the guide to develop you on your skill towards creating the best and touching wedding speech.

Things to Consider

When you are going to write a good wedding speech, you must have some guidelines on how to do it. It must not really be hard but just basic tips to help you in many ways.

Here are the 10 tips that I hope can help you a lot:

Have a plan and simple objective to develop the potential outcome. Imagine the things that you want to get out after giving the speech in front of the people. Do you like to make people laugh? Or touch the emotions of people? Before you write, think of the theme of your speech and visualize what will be the outcome of the things you are going to say.

Your speech must have formal structure with a good beginning, middle an ending. Audience will love to hear a speech that has a map or has sense of direction without drifting off from the topic. You have to welcome and recognize the people attended the wedding. Of course, you have to make the bride and groom the stars.

Do not say too much non-sense. You have to keep speech simple and unique. You can talk for about 5 to 7 minutes to let others also do their parts. Longer than that will just make listeners bored and might find other interests than your speech.

Always talk of positive things. You have to talk only of positive topics and scenario. Do not make any negative comments that will only give negative vibes on a happy celebration. It is a time to celebrate not to put a dark mark on a happy day.

You can research your speech which you can relate on personal stories. The personal stories can help you connect with the audience, especially the bride and groom. You are going to ponder on the beautiful memories you have relating to the celebrant and how you treasure the moments you have with them. How can you relate those stories can be done through searching to work for it positively.

You also have to remember to keep the personal stories short. As much as possible focus the story about the bride and groom because it's not about you. Help people imagine how that moment become so special. Describe it clearly and briefly for them just to grasp enough the event.

Make your opening and closing good. People will mostly remember the speech between the opening and closing. The opening catches the attention of the audience so you need a key to make them want to hear more. The ending will give the inspiration and realization about the speech you have given. It is somewhat the core message you are trying to impart where they can feel emotions about what you have said.

Do not drink alcohol not until you have given your speech. You have to be alert and be yourself while giving the speech. You save yourself drinking alcohol when it is time to celebrate the wedding.

Keep your eyes contact with the audience. If you can sometimes forget your speech, you can use an index card to read the important points of your speech. Just avoid reading throughout the speech and keep your eyes on the audience as much as possible. This is to show that you are sincere on your speech.

Practice makes perfect. Practice your speech and rehearse it in front of someone. You have to get some opinion from others. You can also record the speech and listening back can help you improve your speaking skills and memorize the speech fast.

The Basics of Giving Speech

You may be one of the people who are a first time to give formal speech in front of a large audience. There is a possibility that you are getting nervous now. It is okay for a first timer to feel that way because others who are also giving the same special speeches are nervous. Can you feel your stomach having like small butterflies inside as you are anxious on your part to be called? That is why we must really improve our self-confidence to give a much inspiration speech.

The reason why a person who is giving the speech is because of the wedding crowds waiting for a speech that will not touch only them but most especially to the bride and groom. What you need is to convert your nervous energy into making the most special speech that will touch everybody.

These are some things that you should keep in your mind whenever you are doing a speech in front:

It is not just you that get nervous about public speeches but also everyone who are assigned to do it. It's part of the phobias that people feel around the world. There are even some who are afraid of giving speech than of dying.

The speech is for everyone who is close, supportive and interested people in the wedding ceremony. So, they will be anxious on what you are going to say. The people gathered around the special celebration are there for the union of two people whom they love. They want to hear an inspiration from you and not about your perfect speech. Whatever happens and the content of your speech, they will be proud of you because you tried to inspire them.

When you are writing your speech, think of these things as an inspiration also. Clear message speeches are easier to deliver and less scary to speak. Your audience will also have easier time to listen and very effective as well.

Here are some thoughts of what you can write about your speech to make it easier.

Start with an introduction that can capture their attention. Not only will you be the one to give the speech so make yours unique among others. That is why you need some start off that will trigger interest in their ears. You can start with some personal experience or scenario you encountered with the couple. It's anything that you think that can portrait how much you care for the two for your audience to listen eagerly what will be the next content of your speech.

Once you got their interest, then you will want their full attention throughout your speech. After you got their attention, relate the experience together by giving some inspiring opinion about the personal scenario. Have a map on your speech to where it will be going. You can either make your speech funny or sentimental. You have the choice.

Once there is a map already, you have to follow the direction now to where it will go. You have to make sure that your topic won't go out from the couple who are the stars of the day. People like speeches that are mix funny and sentimental.

Eventually speaking in public is always a scary experience no matter how much you already master the task and effective the tools you are using. What is more important is the way you deliver the speech easily where the keys are there and much better with humor. Just practice and practice and it will be a lot better next time you are invited to have the speech.

Too much time are consumed over speeches and toasts during a wedding ceremony, it makes reassuring when you plan about how to make it through it all. Speeches for best man and maid of honor can be written simply in many ways.

Events such as rehearsal dinners, showers or a bachelor party expect that there will be speeches. So, prepare yourself for appearing always in front of the events.

Take time to think of the things you might consider when you write your different speeches. Since you are expected not only to do it once but many times, you need to plan what you are going to say that really make sense.

Here are some questions that can help you in writing the speech. They are somewhat your guide.

What type of speech you like to do? Is it humorous, sentimental or poetic?

How long does it gonna be?

What is your role on the wedding?

What impression you like to give?

Is this a first or second time wedding?

How long do you know the couple?

How well do you know them?

Do I want the couple to remember my speech?

Take time to answer the following above so you can write a well written speech for the bride and groom. They can also help you think of the inspiration you want to impart that you can include on your speech. Write down each answer before you can start off your best speech. You can eventually edit them as long as you are satisfied already of what you have written.

Here are other questions that might help also:

How did you meet the groom? How long you have known him?

How did you meet the bride and groom? What is your relationship on them before?

How long has been the bride and group a couple?

What are the likes of both?

What are the 5 words that come in your mind when you see them?

What was the funniest thing you have encountered between the couple?

What do you wish for the couple in the future?

These questions can be very important so, you think well. When you have already answered them, it's time that you make a lay out of your speech. This is to put great effort on your important speech and be easier for you.

Starting Your Speech

You cannot start writing your speech when you do not know your subject. Know first what will be the topic of your speech. You must already know it since you are closely related to the bride or groom. You can start the speech about the favorite past memories you have spent. This memory can either be sentimental or funny. Make sure that it's not too personal to share with others.

Also do not forget that you should share a speech that is appropriate for everybody. The next part of your speech is all about the history of the couple, the happy moments of course. Recount the first time that the couple met and fall in love. Also include the other stories that affected both the relationship in a positive way.

If you really want your speech the best one, as early as possible brainstorm your idea so you can formulate the speech. You can use the technique called mind mapping. The technique helps you visualize the presentation you are doing and the structure of the speech. It gives you an easier way to write the speech even on a long form.

When we are old enough after taught to write, we were also taught how to organize the thought we have in writing. We were taught how to write by line from top to bottom. Soon, we are taught how to write a speech, once you have known how to write long paragraphs, with outlines or sub-headings from points to points.

But as of the present, we do not think like that. We do not think anymore of the points or sub-headings. We are now thinking of different ideas in mind. Here are some ideas on how to use mind mapping so you can have a better speech:

You list all your ideas in order to not forget the ideas you have in mind.

Arrange your ideas into a speech from the fragments of the disorganized thoughts.

Edit and eliminate the ideas that are not important.

Applying Mind Mapping to Your Speech

The other way in which you can make your speech is instead of writing it you can create images. In this way your mind maps that you can use as the guide of your speech. The pictures you can convert into sentences.

Here is an overview of how to create mind map:

You can start the mind map by getting a piece of blank paper and a pen, colored pencil or markers.

The topic speech you think must be drawn at the center.

Draw 3 lines that are like a branch from the center. They are for the introduction, main point of your speech and the conclusion.

Each line must have also a symbol or picture so you can easily identify the main point. If you cannot thing of a picture, just put the word.

If you can think of other ideas, you can create other lines as the sub point of your speech.

These are the ways on how to use your mind map for building the speech. The mind mapping can also be use in remembering the family and friends.

To create the actual structure of speech, here are more tips to add on having more information about your speech.

Take your time thinking about your speech. Do not rush making it and not think of what to do. Move your brains and think of what will the people want to know about the bride and groom. Also, you must think of what is the best wish you can give.

Do not be afraid to show your emotion from your speech. It is not wrong to let your true feeling, if you want to cry, then so be it. This is only one chance to talk your true feelings to your friend.

Just be yourself. You will not sincere if you are not being yourself. If you are a humorous person, then make a speech that makes people's stomachache from laughing.

Getting to Know Toasting

When you are getting to have the toast, there are also other things that you should learn. Here is some basic information about toasting that you would like to know.

What is the essential law of toasting? Most of the best toasts are done briefly. Toasting should be because there are many people, not just you, who will be giving the toast. Toasting add a happy mood to the celebration. Eventually, the wedding is all about the bride. This is not about others such as the best man or maid of honor.

Who is the head of rites for toasting? Eventually, the master of the toast is the best man. This is the person who also plans the best bachelor's party for the groom. While the best men spend days and weeks to plan the bachelor's party for the groom, thinking for the toast can be done in one night. So, best man is chosen because he is the best and can deliver good toasts.

Who actually does the toasting? The bride and groom are the one who will select the person to toast and who will have the good impact. This is base on the formality of the wedding and the feelings of all the family. As for the moment, the best man will toast for the bride. As for the groom, the maid of honor will toast for him. Lastly, the father of the bride will toast for the newlywed couple. More toast will come for those who will wish well for the couple.

What is toasting at the rehearsal dinner? People are only thinking about the toasting in wedding that they tend to forget the toasting in rehearsal. The rehearsal dinner gives the opportunity for everyone to share their thoughts with bride and groom on a quiet environment. Also, on the rehearsal dinner is the long toast happens. If you do not want to get pressure on making a wedding toast, then, you can do it during the rehearsal.

When will the toasts happen? For formal weddings, the toast happens after the meal is served. Toast can also be done after the couple slices their wedding cake. To some formal weddings, toasts are done after the couples have their first dance. You can also talk to the caterer to plan the toasting in the right timing.

What do the couples do during the toasts? During the toast, the bride and groom will just smile or say their thanks. They cannot toast their selves eventually. You can go around and return the toasts to everyone, if your wish to.

10 Tips In Toasting for the Weddings

1.   You must ready yourself and be prepared. You have to know who decide the toasting, what order is the toasting and what you will say during the toasting.

2.   You have to be sincere. You have to speak from your heart and use your own words. This is for you to show that you are very sincere about toasting for the couple.

3.   You also have to make it short. You have to make the toast for just two to three minutes. This is because you are not just the one toasting but also many will be next to you.

4.   You have to mind your words. You have to keep the couple from being not embarrass on their most special day. Do not mention something that will mark a not good memory on their wedding day.

5.   Shower compliments as much as possible for the couple. The purpose of the toasts is to say something nice about the couple that you honor.

6.   You can practice the toast on your own in front of the mirrors or someone whom you can ask an opinion. You must make sure that you memorize

the toast you will be doing. You do not really need to use an index card since you will be holding the microphone and the drink.

7.   As much as possible do not drink alcohol after you have made your toast.

8.   You must watch your manner. Just take a small sip on the wine or champagne. Wedding toasts are not about who gets to drink the wine first. Or else you might choke up while doing it.

9.   You have to connect to other people while giving the toast. Eye contact will make you connect with them and speak the words slowly and clearly.

10.   Do not forget to charm the audience. You raise your glass and take a sip at the end of your toast.

To be successful in a wedding toast or speech you have to know the right. It also ensures you to find comfort on doing it.

Some Sample Speeches

Of course, what will be the use of the guide if it does not give some free samples. This section will list some samples that you can get inspiration. So, here they are.

A Sample Speech for Best Man-1

Good morning/afternoon everyone. I am ___ [your name] _. As the best man of [groom's name]. I have known him since [since kids, high school or college]. He is my befriend and the only guy whom I could __[shoot milk out of his nose / play baseball and watch the girls at the same time without missing a pitch.....etc]_____. I still do not forget when we were [something personal memory but keep it clean because audience are listening]. But when he met__[brides name] ___ he totally changes into a new person and would not do again what pranks we used to.

All I can say is that the newlywed couple is very much in love and I wish will have many happy decades as one. I would like to inform the two of them that it was an exceptional tribute for me to be requested to be a part of this happy and memorable day for them both. I and the rest of the people in this wedding party would like to recommend a toast to the happy pair and wish those years upon years of peaceful, joy and our best wishes.

A Sample Speech for Best Man-2

Good /Morning Afternoon Everybody here in this wedding party.

For others who don't know my name, I am _____ and for those of you that do ... well I apologize.

Unwisely, _____ has set me the big tribute of being best man for him on this very exceptional day. Just let me state how thankful I was to have been chosen to talk with you all at such a blissful time, the wedding of _____and _____.

Sadly, those thoughts have now left out the window and I stand here in front of you all ... scared.

Before I pass you to _____, I would like to express my biggest "Thank you" to the bridesmaids because they have done a wonderful work in assisting _____, and look beautiful!

As a matter of fact they are only hidden by _____ herself, who, I'm sure everybody will agree with me that she looks absolutely beautiful in this day. The groom fortunately looks bewildered.

As of the moment, I would like to invite both _(Bride)_____and __(Groom)___ to obtain piece in my speech. Bride will you please place your left/right hand on the table. Groom will you please place your left/right hand on top of Bride's.

Then, I would like to ask a support of you together to remain your hands in this place until the ending of my speech and believe me groom you will be sorry it if you don't.

I am so really, really thankful for finally confessed after all this time that I have known you, that I am the best man!

As an alternative of telling you a lot of stories that can drag on without end, you will have to pay attention to my matrimonial guidance instead. I am not telling that I'm the best person to dish out counsel! Eventually I have the several words of wisdom for the blissful newlywed.

To the Groom;

Primary set the ground system and institute whose chief - then do the whole thing she speaks.

Next, a married life can be compared to a football game ... so, Be Fully Committed Every Week and Make Sure That You Score Every Saturday.

Subsequently, keep in mind the five things; the engagement ring, the wedding ring, the compromising, the children's swing, and the enduring.

Always remember, if you purchase her flowers, she knows you're feeling guilty, and she will bear in mind, to the next, the previous time you bought her some and the reason of what you did.

Finally, here are 3 words you must by no means to overlook, you're right dear.

To the Bride:

This is for you that I have the five key guidelines to a flourishing matrimony.

A gentleman who will care for you good will always stand by your side

A man who will shower you with gifts and respects

A man who will soothe you in times of problems

A man who will give pleasure to you and award you in every demand

Most significantly, make sure ensure that each man would not know the other ones names.

But really _____. You are one fortunate man! You are now married to _____ today.

She's an attractive, stylish, humorous, loving, and kind young woman.

She truly deserves a great partner. I thank God she wedded you before she looked for another one.

Have you still got your hands jointly? .... That is good!

I Spoke To Both ____ And _____ Before The Wedding And I Asked _____ What He Was Looking For In Marriage - He Said "Love, Happiness And Eventually A Family."

When I Asked _____ The Same Question - She Replied - A Coffee Perculator!

Well, She Actually Said A "Perky Copulator" But I Knew What She Meant...

The last and most main chore, of the best man knows when sufficient and enough and I believe that the time has arrived as I gaze down at my girlfriend and see her with her head in her hands, thinking what I have done.

It has been a privilege and honor to be best man of your special day. Once again thanks again for letting me have the opportunity! And I truthfully couldn't hope for a better buddy to be best man for.

I think you will all consent with me that today, _____ truly is the best man and apart from _____ being the most striking person in the room, she is also the luckiest.

In case now that most of you are wondering why I asked _____ to place his hand on top of _____, I will tell you now. _____ as my final role, it has been with great pleasure that I have been able to give you the last five minutes in which you will ever have the upper hand over _____.

Please stand up and raise your glasses to Mr. & Mrs. ******!!!

A Sample Speech for Maid of Honor-1

Good Morning/ Afternoon/ Evening! For those of you who don't know me, I am _____, the very overconfident sister of our stunning Bride. I want to start by cheering the bride and groom, and expressing thanks all the people who came to this special day.

As I gaze at the bride and groom, I can feel mix f emotions. I know that _____ has found her true counterpart and I know that theirs will be a matrimony of everlasting and happy life. My heart is full with love for the couple today. I know you have a fantastic journey in front of you, and with God's blessing your wedding will always be wonderful each year to come.

I, by no means knew _____ before he dated my sister, so I can't tell you horrifying tales about him, but I can tell you that I think he is just right for my sister!? He's easy going, attractive, easy to confide with, and he has a great sense of humor! We are very glad to greet _____ into our family. We know he's made for us, and we hope we're made for him!

_____, I want to note how gorgeous you look today, and to tell you that this has truly been a special day for me. Thank you for giving true meaning to the word sister and for sharing the last 28 years with me. My parents and I have just loved this girl from the day she was born. We've coddled her, liked her, and giggled with her.? I know how much delight she has brought into our lives, and I know that she'll bring that joy into _____ life as well.

As children, _____ and I were attractive much inseparable, and we always handled to keep each other amused. When I think back on our adventures in early childhood days, I have nothing but loving reminiscences. The fondest memoirs include the times we spent at the river containing picnic lunches.

Add a personal memory here, or two etc. To this day, ____ is the simple person I know that can make me chuckle so hard it hurts. I have a lot more humorous and awkward stories about her, but because this is her special day, I will let her pass for once.

I reflected about the words of advice that we'd like to give to the newlyweds and came up with this:

The two secrets of a long permanent and joyful matrimony are a good sense of humor and a short memory!

Always keep in mind to say those three important little words..."You're right dear."

If you're clever, you'll always have the last word. However, if you are very clever, you won't use it.

At any time you are wrong, admit it. Whenever you are right, be quiet.

And, _____, always remember...a happy wife, makes for a happy life!

Independently, you are two extraordinary, extraordinary people, but as one you are whole.

As you sit side by side through this roller coaster of life, remember to scream from the peaks, hold hands through the dips, laugh through the loop the loops, and enjoy every twist and turn.

For the ride is much better when you share it together. Coming together is the beginning; keeping together is progress; working together is success.

I would like to extend a lot of wish to both _____ and _____ that they continue the partnership and love, enjoy laughter. I hope they will be blessed with children and that they always see and talk together with their heart.

The deepest wish I have for you is though many years from now, still the love for each other will be stronger and deepen. Years and decades from now you will look back and remember your wedding day as the day your love is united with each other. I just wish you the best and more love to the both of you.

Everybody raise your glasses because I want to propose a toast to my beloved sister and to her husband:

Live each day and cherish what you have together. Just love one another and stand with each other no matter what happen. Just take time to talk with each other. Always let love and your family be the center of everything. Love like a wind, strong enough to move clouds. But soft enough to never hurt anyone and be happy forever.

Cheers!

A Sample Speech for Maid of Honor-2

Audience fellow members love to pick up about how the match met. In this bridesmaid speech we see how an everyday chance encounter resulted in a lifelong dedication of love.

Introduction

I have known __(Bride)___ for over 10 years and in this time I have come to know that she is many things : caring, loving, sensible, funny, and above all, generous excessively. I couldn't be glad to be here today share out in the joy of her wedlock to Tony.

About the Bride

__ (Bride) ___ and I turned friends when we were both signed up for an evening art class. We quickly learned that natural cycle that age friends do when talking and sharing secrets. Since we were both divorced, we started to get our kids together on the weekends for playfulness fields day at the zoo and things like that. Our friendship turned one of the most really important of my life. I could tell Julia anything and everything and realize that there wasn't a judgmental bone in her body.

About the Relationship

About three years ago I won tickets to an ice hockey. I had never been to one and asked Julia if poured forth wants to go with me. Thinking of her kids first, she was hesitant, but I finally talked her into it. We shared a babysitter and went out for a midnight of fun, not being totally sure that this would be the night she would meet Tony. He was there with his oldest son and they struck up a conversation at the yielding stand. When she came back to our seats she had a HUGE smile on her face. I told her she look. I shared with her she resemble the cat that ate the canary and she just pulled in a sheet out of her pocket and evinced it to me. I remember look the numbers and wondering what she was showing me when she just said, His name is Tony. I started expressing joy and was so happy for her. Who knew that standing in line to get a pretzel could be so fruitful?

Conclusion

Some years ago an art teacher provided me this quotation from Marc Chagall. In our life there is a single color, as on an artist's palette, which supplies the significance of life and art. It is the color of love. Julia and Tony, I hope that the house painting of your life is colored by not a single thing but love! Cheers to the bride and groom!

Bride's Sample Speech

Friends and family I'd care to thank all of you for being here at some point, particularly since the majority of you knew that I'd want to say a few words it's very impacting that you still decided to come.

From the moment we got engaged I've been thinking about this wedding ceremony. I just wanted the whole thing to be perfect and was ascertained not to look out over even the most unimportant detail. But I needn't have worried, his best man includes the accessories he was there.

I'm so glad to be wed to Paul; caring, talented, meek, charming I can see why he selected me. Earnestly, I don't believe there could ever be anyone in this world more suitable for me than Paul is and I apprize my good fortune in getting married to such a warm-hearted and loving man. When we first led off going out together I was drawn in by his dream, drive and. determination. Three years later, when he declared oneself to me, I earned that without those qualities our matrimony will still be as powerful and I'd love him even as much. Paul brings out the favorable in me, he makes me laugh and he makes me enjoy each and every instant of life just by to be a part of mine. They tell that you don't marry someone you can live with you splice the one who you cannot hold up without. This is certainly true with Paul, I simply couldn't live without him and I look forward to maturity.

But lots of people look to think there is a large difference to your marital life once you are married. Someone told me that previous to marriage a man will lay awake all night contemplate something you told, while after matrimony he'll fall asleep ahead of you have completed saying it. Well, Paul has talked to me about union you bet life is going to change. He talked about the hours ahead of the kitchen sink, the rinsing of socks, unpaid secretary, social organizer, babysitter, cook, etc.

This evening would not have gone nearly so well without the generous help of so many people and whilst my better half has already taken care of the thank you, I would like to single out a few of you for my own kudos.

Firstly, my marvelous mother who has been a tower of strength over the last eight months and the stone of the substructure on which this whole day seemed to be made. In my life she has made me very felicitous and I must take this chance to thank her not only for her wearing and mostly.

Moving on to my father, who wanted to give me the big event of my aspirations and followed. I understand there was a bet going on as to whether he would have tears in his eyes when he walked me down the aisle today. He did have tears in his eyes, but that might have been because he was interesting over what he would say to his bank manager on Monday morning. My dad is an unnerving quality as well as a adoring family man. We are very nigh and, unsurprisingly, given his spirit, his unselfishness and his, I've constantly looked up to him. It would definitely take quite man to live up to my father, but in Paul, I have learned that man.

There are other parents I want to thank too my partner, for their generous share and their uninterrupted support in the lead up to the wedding. Sally and Ray made me feel so welcome right from the very first time I met them and I feel vastly giving to have married into such a great family. My sincere wish is that together Paul and I can make a place that is as welcoming and as full of love and happiness as theirs is – personally speaking I also quite like the idea of five bedrooms, three bathrooms and a big garden too.

Of course, I have another special reason to thank Sally and Ray – their care and guidance over the years has had a very positive influence over Paul and their very best qualities have rubbed off on him. They raised him so he'd grow up to be a perfect husband. Look how well he did today saying, 'I do' at the right place in the ceremony. As long as he keeps saying 'Yes dear' we'll have a wonderful marriage.

Our encouraging cast merits acknowledgement too. And they are all of Paul's brothers, Gary, Richard and Mark our ushers. Paul's best man and best friend, Jason depending on the substances of his speech they might even stay friends. My bridesmaids, Helen and Liz who have been a wonderful help to me, not only today, but throughout the various weeks of vivid wedding readiness. And last but not least, I'd like to generate a exceptional mention of Lucy, my chief maid of honor. She is the unsung heroine of this nuptials, whilst not all her endeavor at some point would not have been half as enjoyable for me. She is my oldest and dearest friend and we have been during some bad times and we have been through a good deal of good times. Her friendship has been a source of strength to me throughout the years and I experienced rewarded to have her standing with me today.

Lastly, let me end as I began, by thank you all once more for following tonight. I can frankly say that tonight would not have been the very same if we had not been together with our dearly friends and family. At weddings it is the strangers that create the party ambiance and you good people have for certain done that for us. May I suggest a toast to love, laughter and friendship.

Cheers!

Grooms Sample Speech

On behalf of my wife and I, we'd like to thank you all for arriving here tonight and sharing our exceptional day with us. There are times when it's beneficial to be surrounded by people who are important to you, and for us this is one of those socials function. We hope that you're reveling it as much as we are and we'd like to thank you for your kind wishes well cards, presents and support.

We are required to say we've been really affected by the number of individuals that have tantalized round to help us in preparedness for today, if you're not referred by name and that's most of you, delight feel comfortable knowing that Kate and I are very grateful.

David and Maggie, thank you not only for your hospitality tonight and your benignity, but for also presenting me your very utterly divine daughter. I promise I'll take good care of her and naturally do almost everything she tells me to, even if it involves golf! I must concede I did actually try it a while ago, and during one lesson with the hometown pro I asked him whether he had seen any advance since my last moral. And he said er yup, that's a any better haircut.

So Maggie, we have a personal gift here for you.

I also desire to say thank you to my parents who put up with me for all these years, you have both been there for me when I've needed you and given me a marvelous start in life and I 'm very endowed and proud to have you as my mum and dad. I've a gift idea for you here Mum, as a thank you. I can visualize that Neil, my best man is getting raring to make his speech soon. Now many more people don't know that Neil is suffering from a uncommon medical status which makes him to fabricate notional stories. He really does consider these stories to be true and I thank you for humoring him during his speech.

I am utterly beguiled to be able stand here tonight with Kate, I never knew what was missing in my life before I met her. Kate has been at root age of friendship, support and love. Of course I've to be sure that she is going to tell me after that the only matter losing in my life at the moment is golf, even though I am still watching for her to explain the attraction to a game that comprises of much of walking, broken up by letdown and bad arithmetic. And finally, the bridesmaids, thanks for calming Kate nerves and aiding in her planning today. I'd also like thank you for getting her to the church without hassle and on time, you've done a brilliant job. We have a small gift for each of you as a token of our admiration.

Well, that's it from me for now, but, before I go across you over to my best man, Ladies and Gentlemen, please stand and lift your glasses and join me in a toast to maids of honor...

Father of the Bride Sample Speech

Ladies and gentlemen, as father of the bride, it's my privilege to make the first speech, and I'd like to start by telling what a pleasant it is to welcome you all to Karen and Peters wedding.

I want to welcome Peters parents, Pauline and Alan, and all the relatives and friends of both families, and to thank you all for arriving, peculiarly those of you who have moved around great lengths to be here today. It's excellent to see you all.

These days, we on the top table are environed by most of the friends and family who have been expected to us during our lives. And by your presence today, you show your friendship and love, and bring even greater joy to this grand day.

Sorry to say, we are missing two very significant people however Karen's Nanna and Grand-dad, who were not capable to make the trip due to Grand-dads unhealthiness. We will be making a special journey north tomorrow to show them Karen in her bridal gown, and take them some scenes of the day and some cake. Meanwhile, I would be thankful if you will raise your glasses in their honor - to Nanna and Grand-dad. Thank you.

I'm also very happy to officially welcome Peter into the family, even though, as far as we're concerned, he's been part of the family for ages. During the time that we have known Peter, we have delivered to agonize just how exceptional he is to Karen anyone can see that they're made for each other. I'm sure you'll agree they make a beautiful couple.

A great deal of effort has gone into making this the special day that Karen and Peter merit, and I'd like to make peculiar mention of a few of the people referred. Peter's parents, Pauline and Alan have made a big part towards the achievements of today, and I'd like to thank them for all their tries. Also, Karen and Peter themselves have done work hard, and with great keenness to make the necessary agreements, especially for the honeymoon, which seems to have been a little of a top priority! I'd also like to thank the staff of the Parsonage for helping to make this a special day.

And there's another person who has worked inexhaustibly over many months to develop the handmade invitations, the Orders of Service, and the menu cards, which I'm sure you'll agree were fab. Also, her talents extended to preparing all the candelabras that you see prior to you. She would tell that it was a labor of love, and I know how much Karen and Peter take account her efforts, but I'd like add my thanks and suggest a toast to the mother of the bride to Susan.

I am really fortunate that my daughter has met her Mr. Right. Of course, marriage isn't just about finding the perfect partner, but also about being one. Karen has made such a success of her life and career so far, that I'm sure her marriage to Peter will be just as successful.

I am really endowed that my daughter has met her Mr. Right. Of course, wedlock isn't about discovering the perfect married person, but also about being one. Karen has made such a success of her life and career so far, that I'm sure her union to Peter will be even as successful.

Susan and I have been desiring this day for a long time not because we want to give over responsibility for our daughter, but basically because it's a proud day for us to see Karen so felicitous, so in love and looking so beautiful today.

But passing on Karen over to Peter reminds me of that well known hypothesis about wedlock:

If you love something, set it free.

If it comes back, it was, and will always be yours.

If it never returns, it was never yours to begin with.

And if all it does is sit in your house, mess up your stuff, spend your money and use the telephone all night you either married it or gave birth thereto.

Spousal relationship is a comical thing though. Did you know that in a recent sight carried dead set launch whether hubby live longer than bachelors, they learned that in reality there's no divergence. It just seems longer when you're married!

Peter made an existent opinion on me when he first came into Karen's life. It was about two in the morning, and he was lying in the gutter outside our house next to a speed bump singing Angels to. Karen, with Andy attempting to shut him up. Pity Karen wasn't at home that night to take accounts it.

But Peter's an outstanding fella, only problem with him is he's an Arsenal fan, but even Gooners deserve a chance in life and marrying into a Chelsea family gives him an opportunity to see the light before his life is totally ruined.

Peter will know by now that Karen's not the shy, retiring type - she likes to be the center. That's in all probability why she took to dancing from an original age she joined a dance school at the age of three and I didn't see her again until she was18, still, it kept her out of trouble.

She's also very substantial willed, as Peter will have investigated, and we've had many a battle of wills over the years. Susan opines that's because were overmuch alike, but I think she takes after.

Seriously though, I know that Karen and Peter will be as happy as Susan and I are, and can look forward to many happy years together.

Karen is a very caring and loving person. She's my only daughter, and I love her and I'm very proud to have her as my daughter.

Please join me in raising your glasses in a toast to the happy couple – Karen & Peter.

I'd now like to hand over to my son-in-law – Peter.

Wow, what an emotional wedding – even the cake's in tears!

Father of the Groom Sample Speech

"Good morning/afternoon/evening, everyone. It is with great joy that I welcome you all to my son, __(Groom's name)__ and __(Bride's name)__ wedding. We also bid a big welcome to (bride's name) family. A festivity of a new chapter in life like this will never be celebrated alone. My wife and I are happy to have you all with us. Standing here today, I'm inundated with images of my son as a baby boy and a boy eager to go to school. During those finite instants, I was a very proud father. For dinner, I have the image of my son as a man, off to start a new option in life with his beautiful wife, (bride's name). And I am proudest I have ever been. (Brides name), it was terrific getting to know you over these few months' years and were so happy to know how favorable our son is to have you. We formally receive you into our family and we are even more enthralled that your whole family can celebrate this wondrous party with us. Truly, this is a joyous day. You start your life as a marriage this evening and while it's going to be an experience which will teach you lots of things, let me offer you with a little bit of advice. A bit of advice. Matrimonial lifespan is not all peaches and cream and it won't all be fun times but even throughout the hard knocks and challenges, you've promised to stay together and as you stay together, keep on loving each other. With so many potential misdirection with life like work, it's easy to lose sight of what's important but the bottom line is your love for each other is the most crucial. Family and friends let us now drink a toast to the love, the health, and the paradise of (groom's name, bride's name.)"

Mother of the Bride Sample Speech

Today we are honored to celebrate the marriage of our daughter Mary to her groom, Jim. There are much of familiar fronts out there, and I want to inform you all how pleased we are to welcome you here today.

Mary, I love you and I count on you have a marriage as fulfilling and rattling as the one your mother and I have enjoyed throughout the years. Marriage is a long term commitment, yes -- but during the good and the bad, it's such a thanksgiving to have the love of your life standing by your side. I find that you and Jim will honor and value the covenant of wedlock that you've got in into today and have every year of love and paradise ahead.

Jim, we know you will take good care of our girl. She's a feisty one, that's for sure. But she's also enjoying and giving care, and I know the two of you will be very felicitous together. It is with great joy that we welcome you to our family on this particular day.

With no more extra commotion, I'd like everyone to raise your glasses in honor of the bride and groom - here's to many years of love and laughter ahead!

Mother of the Groom Sample Speech

To my wondrous son, Henry and his bride Karen. I am so swept over with emotions right now. On the one hand I'm over the moon about the two of you being married that I just don't have quite an accurate words to explain it. Then again, today brings to light the fact that my son is grown up. I mean, he's been grown up awhile, but it's with so different notions when one of your children is married. I knew this day would come and I believed I was prepared for it, I was even who is fit at the rehearsal. But when the music started playing and Karen was stride down the aisle, I looked back at Henry and saw the large smile on your face. I just lost it. You two mimic you were ready to take on the world and you still do. I can feel safe that you'll take good care of each other and will be happy united.

Henry, I've loved you since the minute I heard we were anticipating you and I'll stay on love you for the rest of my life. I'm so pleased you and I look forward to seeing what the succeeding holds for you. You know I'm still here and will forever be here if you ever need anything.

To Karen, your love thoroughly gorgeous and I see myself lucky to have you for a daughter in law. You're everything a mother surely could need for her son and it's been so great getting to know you.

Now before I tear up again, I'd like to toast the bride and groom. Congratulations and God bless you both.

Examples of Wedding Toast

Sample of Best Man Wedding Toast to the Groom

Here is to my friend. Today I had the honor to stand beside him on this most important day, as he has so often stood by me in good times and bad.

I wish him and his lovely bride nothing but happiness, prosperity, and good health for as long as they shall live.

Sample Maid of Honor Wedding Toast to Couple

It can be hard to share your best friend with someone else, but I have been thrilled to share (Bride) with (Groom.)

The love you show to each other is inspiring and beautiful and I look forward to seeing it continue to grow.

I am honored to be able to raise a toast to my wonderful best friend and her new husband.

To (Bride) and (Groom)!

Sample Bride Wedding Toast to Groom

To my wonderful new husband, who has shown me what love really is.

Who is the reason for my happy days and the comfort in my sad ones.

Who cheers my successes and comforts me in my failures.

I am so proud to be your wife. I love you. Cheers!

Sample Groom's Toasts - From Groom to Bride's Parents

I raise my glass and ask you to join me in a toast to the parents of my lovely bride.

They must have done a lot of things right to raise such a beautiful and gifted daughter as my Bride.

I promise to live up to the trust they have placed in me, and I thank them from the bottom of my heart.

Sample Bridesmaid Toast to Couple

To (Bride) and (Groom), may your winters be full of twinkling white lights, may your springs be full of freshly picked flowers, may your summers be full of bright blue oceans and may your autumns be full of warm cups of tea.

May each day you spend together be full of the small things that make life wonderful.

Sample Father of the Bride Wedding Toast to Bride

Let us raise our glasses and toast the happy couple.

The bride has been like a ray of warm sun light on my soul from the day she was born.

Now, she begins a new life and there will be another man to whom she will turn for love and protection.

But I want her to know her father will always be there for her. Cheers.

Sample Sister of Bride Wedding Toast to the Couple

I've been so fortunate to spend my life with such a wonderful sister and I'm thrilled today to add a new brother to our family.

May the love you share today grow throughout the years. Welcome to the family, (Groom's name).

Please raise your glass to my sister and my new brother in law.

Sample Brother of the Bride Wedding Toasts

"I toast my sister to honor her wedding day, but more important in memory of the years we have spent together. My heart is filled with unspeakable pride. The memories of all we shared will be with me always. I love you, sister, you will be part of my life forever."

Do's and Don'ts

If you are going to give a speech there are also certain rules such as what you should not do and what you should do. Here are the do's and don'ts when giving a wedding speech:

If you are the best man, don't forget that the speech should not be an extension of what happened last night. Make sure that you do not talk of vulgarity and bad language.

Do try to make your speech sincere. Though many would think that it's corny but when it comes to wedding event, it is an emotion that is expected.

Do take with you your index card in case you forgot your speech.

Do try to relax yourself and take a long breath so you forgot your nervousness.

Do try to start with a speech that is either funny or witty. Once you make the audience laugh, it will be easy for you to deliver the speech.

Do have self-confidence and look around the people while you are giving the speech. Let the people think you are relax and confident.

Don't mumble on your speech. In case there is no microphone speak loudly and clearly.

Do wait for a while until everyone has already stood up when you are making a toast. Raise your hands into the air and also wait for everybody to do the same too.

Don't use photo or props and pass it over to all people. This will only lead to people's attention to what you have given.

How to Present Your Wedding Speech

Now that you know the way to write your speech, it is time for you to know now how to present them to the audience. There are many approaches that you can do and here are some of them:

Be familiar on the environment. You have to check the room where you are going to conduct your speech. Check the microphone and other device that will be used. Greet the people who are present in the wedding and build a connection with them.

Think and mind your attitude while speaking. It will not be helpful if you will think something negative such as you cannot make it or you cannot do it. Think positive so you can deliver the speech also in a positive way.

Do not forget to smile. Everybody will look while you are talking. Look confident and smile to everyone. This is a happy moment and smiling will lift everybody's spirit.

Connect with your audience. Do not forget to look in the eyes of everybody. This is for them to feel that you are sincere on what you are talking.

Speak with at ease. As much as possible you have to speak on your own and not relying on your notes. Just speak as if you are talking to someone. Be just yourself and speak with humor.

In this way, you will be remembered by everybody because of your memorable speech.

The Ten Commandments of Toasting

Just plan to chat for about 1 to 4 minutes. No one would like to hear a long toast and eventually people will get bored. The important thing is whether long or short, you have delivered your toast speech sincerely and with feelings.

Make sure that all the glasses of people are full before you start your toast. You can say to the guests or the MC to fill their glasses because you will be toasting. You can give 3-5 minutes for the task.

Stand in the entire crowd when you are giving the toast and then raise your right hand holding the glass. It is traditional that after giving the toast glasses should be clink together before you sip.

You can start the toast speech with something personal. It can be how the bride and groom met. You can make the talk with humor as a start.

Humor is always a good taste. You can have some fun with the bride and groom but not too much. This is because they might find it offending.

Just speak with your normal voice. Do not try something not natural or having accents which make the speech unclear. Guests want to hear all the things you want to say.

Before the wedding, you can practice the toast. This is most vital if you are not an accomplish public speaker.

You have to have connection with the people who are looking at you, especially the bride and groom. Do not forget to have an eye contact.

Speak slowly and clearly. Do not rush your toast. Just take a deep breath because if you speak too fast people will not hear what you say.

Lastly, you have to finish your toast with a blessing, congratulation, wish and cheers.

How to Deal With Anxiety

The anxiety you have while having speech is not actually a fear but a phobia. Each person experiences this kind of thing but eventually we can do things to get it control. Here are the things on how you deal your anxiety:

The audience or attendees in the wedding party you do not know mostly, so, since you are just doing this once why not make it worth.

Just have time to get to know the people in the reception. The more you know about them the more you can have confident while making your speech.

Just select the fit speech for you. This is because if you are comfortable with your topic, the less anxious you will feel. Choose the topic in which appropriate to the couple which you will be talking and wishing about.

If you practice perfectly your speech, you can do the delivery like what you have practiced.

Have an organized note so you can't go wrong in delivering them.

Have confidence when you are giving your speech. Just imagine yourself giving the speech with high head.

Just prepare if anything go wrong in your plan. You have to create plan B.

Take a deep breath before you give your speech. Learn techniques on how to relax before you give the speech.

Present yourself at the best. If you are not looking physically well, you cannot perform mentally well too. Take a goodnight sleep before you make the speech so you can relax your mind.

Keep your head on the speech not on the feelings you have, especially on the anxiety.

Having mistakes are okay as long as you continue on your speech and not dwell on them. This will only create more anxiety.

Look each face on the crowd with smile. You must have an eye contact so that they will feel your message. If you smile, it is sure that they will smile back to you.

Possible Topics

Before you can write your speech, of course you need to have a topic. This is what your speech will be all about. Here are some of the topics that you can write about on your speech:

Congratulations Theme- this is a speech centered on pure congratulation to the success of the wedding and especially to the bride and groom. You need to enumerate the reasons why you are happy and excited for the couple's marriage.

Humor Theme- this is a speech that you make your audience laugh about something to the bride and groom. But mind what your joke so you will not create disapproving feeling towards the ambiance of the ceremony. Just speak something witty that does not go over their heads.

Personal Theme- this is a topic that mostly used by parents or other close family of the bride and groom. This often contains advices from their close loved ones and the mistake they should avoid as being a married couple. This theme is either funny or sentimental.

Poetic Theme - this is a speech that may contain reading a poem at the beginning. This poem applies to the newlywed couple and about the marriage life.

Conclusion

In a wedding having wedding speeches is normal and traditional part of the ceremony. Most close people do this task to congratulate and wish the couple of the new stage they have made in life. By following the guidelines above, I am sure you are one of those people who will give the best speech to the bride and groom. Make your speech remarkable that will be remembered by everybody.

Speeches are given at any time. They can do it before the food is served or after everybody is already mingling. Just know your timing when to give and be confident of what you have to say. That is why practicing your speech makes it perfect. The speech can also be lead to a wedding toast for the bride and groom.

Now, with the tips mentioned, I hope you will not be nervous as to what past experience you have about speeches.

You can now create your own unique, funny or sentimental speech that people will remember, especially the bride and groom. Make this once in a lifetime experience for the couple worth remembering.